# Brett and the Magic Super Heroes

## By Sandi Bloomberg

### Illustrated by Kevin Scott Collier

**This book is dedicated to my grandson Brett who loves all super heroes.  In fact, he is *my* super hero!**

ACKNOWLEDGEMENTS

To my husband Jerry, my three sons, Ronny, Lee, and Michael, my three daughters-in-law, Donna, Jackie, and Renee, and my six grandchildren, Corey, Ethan, Brett, Ava, Jake, and Veronica, for their continued love and support.

To my illustrator Kevin Scott Collier for his vision, talent, and imaginative illustrations, and to Lisa at Halo, for all of her personal input and patience.

---

**For more information, contact:** Sandi Bloomberg
Email Author at: Harvela16@aol.com   •   Website: www.sandibloomberg.com
Library of Congress Control Number: 2009934107
ISBN 978-1-935268-17-8

Halo
Publishing International
www.halopublishing.com

Printed in the United States of America

Brett loved super heroes.  He kept a collection of them on a shelf in his bedroom.  He even had super hero books and games.

Brett's mother bought him Cricketman bed sheets and Flyman pajamas. His father bought him a Powerman scooter.

The day before his birthday, Brett watched "Flyman," his favorite program on television.  Brett wished that he had the same magical powers as the boy on the t.v. show, who was able to bring "Flyman" to life.

That night, Brett made a special birthday wish, to wake up with magical powers.

The next morning, he woke up a bit
disappointed.  It was his birthday, but
he did not notice any magical powers.
Little did he know....

Brett's Aunt Fran came to his house to take him to the local toy store to pick out a birthday present.

"You can pick out any action figure you want," said his aunt. "I know that's what you want, but I didn't know which one to buy for you."

As soon as they entered the store, Brett went right to the aisle with the action heroes.  Aunt Fran, still watching over Brett, went to the next aisle to look at the books.

Brett picked up the box with Flyman in it. All at once, the figure, in a muffled voice said, "I love you, Brett."

"Choose me," said Powerman.

"Please take me home," said Cricketman.

Brett watched in amazement as the figures began to break out of their boxes to fly onto his shoulder.

"You're the only one who understands us," said Rangerman.

"Only you can take care of us," said The Bulk.

"Yikes!" said Brett as more figures began to break out of their boxes screaming "Choose me!  Choose me!"

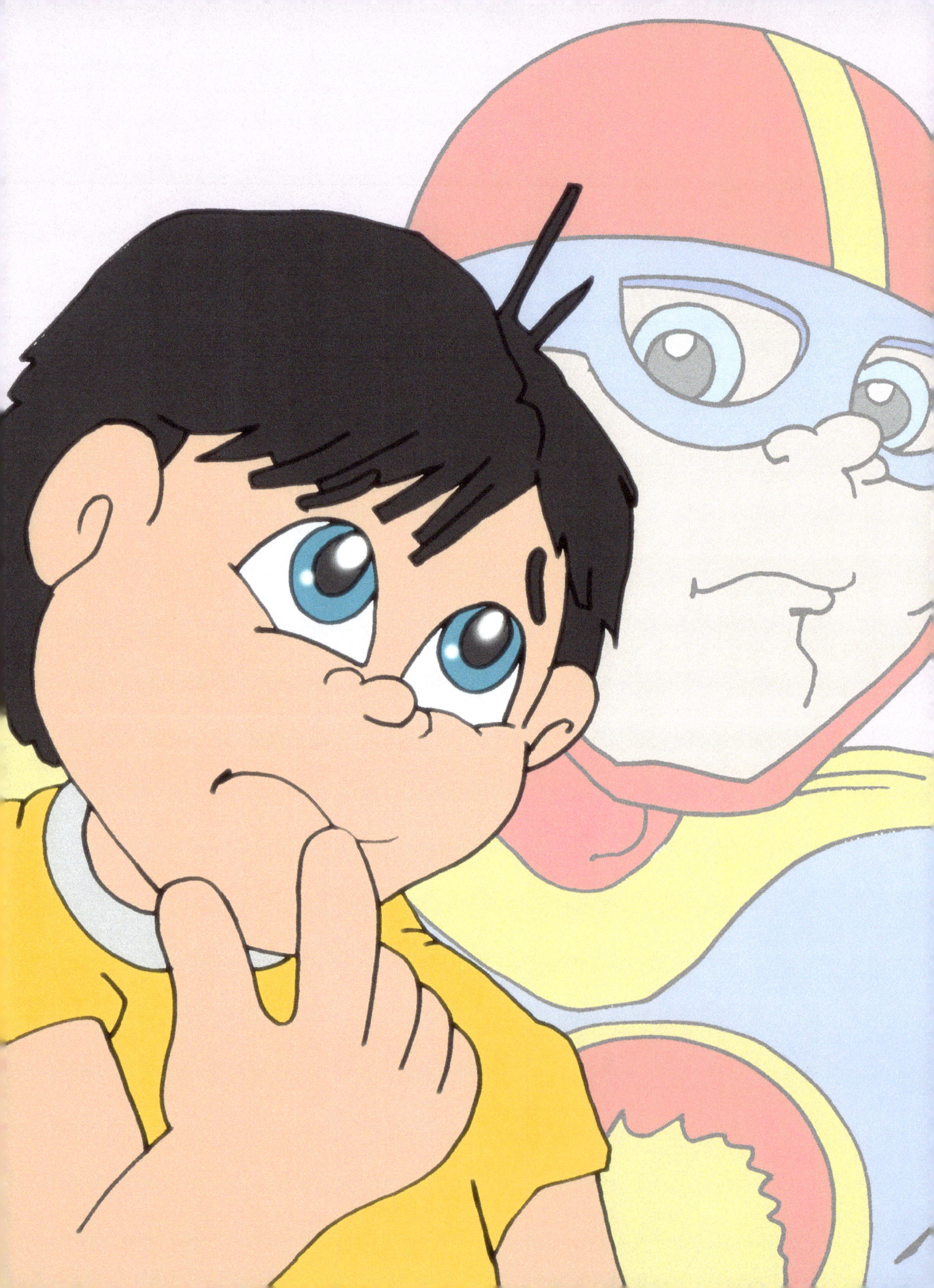

Brett knew at once that his wish was coming true, but now he was having second thoughts about having magical powers.

Before the action figures caused a riot in the store, Brett quickly put them back into their boxes on the shelf and hurried over to his aunt in the next aisle.

She was still looking at books when Brett approached her and said, "Aunt Fran, I decided that I would rather have a board game.

"That's fine dear, but what made you change your mind?"

"It's a long story, Aunt Fran," said Brett as they walked to the section of the store with board games.

Brett could have sworn he heard a super hero yell out to him, "Maybe next time, Brett!"